He wasn't there.

She looked under the bed.

He wasn't there.

The BUNNY That Couldn't Be FOUND

By Angela Mitchell

Illustrated by Sarah Horne

As Johnny Bunny slipped through his doggy flap,
Princess Lolly yawned and stretched.

"Mmm, what a lovely dream. Johnny Bunny," she
called, sweetly. "Where is my adorable pooch?"

She looked under the covers.

She looked in
the royal closet.

He wasn't
there either.

She flung open the windows and looked all around her kingdom.

Johnny Bunny wasn't
anywhere to be seen.

"Bunny is missing!" she screamed.
"Oh, where can he be?"

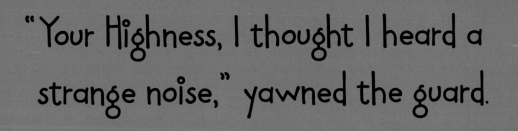

"Your Highness, I thought I heard a strange noise," yawned the guard.

"My Bunny is missing. Johnny Bunny has gone. Call the sergeant pronto!" ordered Princess Lolly. "The palace *must* be searched."

"Your Highness, we've been informed that your pet has gone missing. What are we looking for?"

"Bunny," sobbed Princess Lolly, "Johnny Bunny."

"Can you describe him, Your Highness?" said the sergeant.

"He's white, with an adorable black patch over one eye," sobbed Princess Lolly.

"Here bunny, bunny!" They called.
"He's not here Sarge."

Johnny Bunny wondered why
they were calling his name

and so followed them to
the throne room...

"Bunny...sweet, adorable bunny." On hearing the sergeant's loving tone, Johnny Bunny tried a few of his cute tricks.

"Pesky dog," growled the sergeant, and pushed Johnny Bunny away.

"Bunny... Here bunny, bunny!"

Could a tasty morsel be on offer? On hearing his name again, Johnny Bunny ran, lost his grip and slid along the shiny ballroom floor, slamming into the search party.

"Will someone please remove this pesky dog!" shouted the sergeant.

Johnny Bunny fled to the safety of the kitchen.

"Animals? In my kitchen?! Never. Never!" flustered the cook.

Johnny Bunny couldn't understand why these grumpy fellows were *still* calling his name, but ignoring him. Not even a bone or a tasty morsel. NOTHING.

Aaaaaaaaaooooooooooo!

"Here, bunny, bunny." Johnny Bunny sidled up to the sergeant once more. "Pesky mutt! You're hampering our investigation!"

As they entered the garden, the sergeant ordered: "Search the carrots! Lift every leaf! Pull them up if you have to. I WANT THAT RABBIT FOUND!"

"Yes, Sarge," sighed the policemen.

Poor Johnny Bunny. He was tired and hungry, and a little dizzy with all the toing and froing, so he decided to return to the royal bedroom for a little nap.

"Bunny! My Bunny. Johnny Bunny is back!" The Princess's cry could be heard throughout the palace. The guard, the sergeant and all the policemen came rushing in.

"My - Bunny's - back," sobbed Princess Lolly.
"But *that's* not a rabbit," said the sergeant, confused.
"Quite," said the guard.

The Bunny That Couldn't Be Found

An original concept by author Angela Mitchell

© Angela Mitchell

Illustrated by Sarah Horne

Published by MAVERICK ARTS PUBLISHING LTD

The Studio, Ashley House, Swan Corner, Pulborough, West Sussex, RH20 1AH

© Maverick Arts Publishing Limited July 2013 +44 (0) 1798 875980

A CIP catalogue record for this book is available at the British Library.

ISBN 978-1-84886-108-4